# TOM'S HATS

## ANDRE AMSTUTZ

BLue Bananas

For Aaron
—And his many hats—

# TOM'S HATS

## ANDRE AMSTUTZ

MAMMOTH

First published in Great Britain 1996
by W H Books Ltd and Mammoth, imprints of Reed International Books Ltd
Michelin House, 81 Fulham Road, London SW3 6RB
and Auckland, Melbourne, Singapore and Toronto
10 9 8 7 6 5 4 3
Text and illustrations copyright © André Amstutz 1996
The author has asserted his moral rights
Paperback  ISBN 0 7497 1830 7
Hardback ISBN 0 434 97456 0
A CIP catalogue record for this title
is available from the British Library
Produced by Mandarin Offset Ltd
Printed and bound in China

Tom collected hats.

He kept them in a basket

in his bedroom.

Tom and his sister, Emma,

were getting ready for school.

Their dog, Jasper, was with them.

On the way to school

Tom and Emma met

Fred Potter and his gang.

Tom was wearing his

fireman's hat.

6

The gang made fun of him

and Tom felt silly. So he

took off his fireman's hat.

When Mr Peck, the lollipop man,

gave him a smile,

he felt better.

He put his hat

back on again.

At school, Tom and Emma

liked the Art Class best.

Tom made another hat

and Emma painted it.

Fred Potter and his gang

made a lot of noise.

At the end of the lesson,

they had not made anything –

except a lot of mess.

Back home, Tom showed

his mum his hat.

Tom wore his hat all through tea.

He even wore his hat in bed!

On board the SEA SPRAT,

Tom was giving orders.

A great storm had blown up

and the little boat

tossed and turned.

Then, at last,

the sea was calm

and the sun came out.

Emma called from the crow's nest.

They tied up the boat and

unloaded a rope,

a shovel,

a torch

and the basket

of hats.

14

Jasper began to bark.

He ran up some steps.

Tom and Emma

chased after him.

16

They got to the top of the steps

and there was the treasure.

But three fierce monsters

stood in front of it.

Thinking quickly, Emma shouted:

'Fetch the magician's hat!'

And, just in time,

Jasper came back with

the right hat.

Tom put it on and shouted

the magic word.

There was a big flash

and a lot of orange smoke.

Abracadabra!

Where the three fierce monsters

had stood, there were now

three large pelicans.

When the last piece of treasure

was loaded, they all flew

back to the SEA SPRAT.

Once safely on board,
they unloaded the treasure
and had a party.

There were

fishcakes

for the

pelicans

and chocolate

cream cakes

for Tom and

Emma.

Jasper ate both.

Suddenly there was a shout

and the SEA SPRAT

began to rock.

The pelicans flew away in fright.

Tom rushed on deck to see a

nasty looking pirate and his crew.

'Get the hat box!' shouted Emma.

'It's down below,' said Tom.

And they ran down

into the cabin.

Tom pulled some space helmets

from the basket.

As they put them on, there was
a whirring and a buzzing and
WHOOSH...the boat became
a spaceship!

They flew past

a million twinkling stars

and a million planets.

At last they saw the bright

silvery glow of Moon City.

Tom pressed the landing button

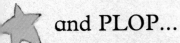

and PLOP...

the space ship landed

right in the middle of

Half Moon Square.

Walking down Full Moon Street,

Emma saw CRATER CAFE.

She felt very hungry.

They went inside and ordered

Moonburgers and Lunar Ices.

They had no money,

but the waitress said she would

take treasure.

Suddenly, bright lights

shone from above.

Tom and Emma ran back

to the space ship, jumped inside

and slammed the door shut.

But before they could press the

TAKE OFF button, the space ship

was sucked up into a huge craft.

We want the treasure. Get it **now**!

They were taken to the control room where a fierce alien and his gang came towards them.

Quickly, Tom reached for the

hat basket, but it was too late.

The aliens had found the treasure!

The fierce alien pulled a lever
and Emma, Tom and Jasper
fell through a trap door
into the inky space.

Over and over they tumbled

in the endless dark space.

Then it began to get lighter

and with a SWISH

and a FLOP, they landed

on a pile of straw bales.

The sun was shining,

the birds were singing,

and the church bells were ringing.

They seemed to be safe,

but where were they?

Tom pulled a hat from

the basket and put it on.

It was his Zoo Keeper's hat.

Soon they heard all the noises

of early morning at the zoo.

They met the Elephant Keeper

and Emma told her they were lost.

'Give me your address,' she said,

'and Jumbo will take you home.'

41

The elephant knelt down

so that Tom and Emma

could climb onto his back.

Jasper took a flying leap

and landed next to them.

Gently the elephant stood up

and they were on their way home.

People stared as the elephant

walked down the High Street

with a boy, a girl, a dog

and a basket of hats

on his back!

43

44

When they reached home,

Emma and Tom slid off

the elephant's back

and ran inside.

They just had time

to have breakfast

and get ready for school.

Which hat should Tom wear?

At last, Tom chose his School cap.

He was looking forward to doing

sums and writing. Maybe

later, in the Art Class, he

could make another hat!